For Fran Manushkin

VIKING
Published by the Penguin Group
Penguin Putnam Books for Young Readers, 345 Hudson Street, New York, New York 10014, U.S.A.
Penguin Books Ltd, Registered Offices: Harmondsworth, Middlesex, England

First published in 1969 in the United States of America by The Macmillan Publishing Company
Published in 1998 by Viking and Puffin Books,
divisions of Penguin Putnam Books for Young Readers

10 9 8 7 6

LIBRARY OF CONGRESS CATALOGING-IN-PUBLICATION DATA
Keats, Ezra Jack.
Goggles! / Ezra Jack Keats.
    p.   cm.
Summary: Two boys must outsmart the neighborhood
bullies before they can enjoy their new treasure, a pair of
lensless motorcycle goggles.
ISBN 978-0-670-88062-1 — ISBN 978-0-14-056440-2 (pbk.)
[1. Bullies—Fiction. 2. City and town life—Fiction.
3. Afro-Americans—Fiction.] I. Title.
PZ7.K2253Go 1998 [E]—dc21 97-47433 CIP AC

Manufactured in China
Set in Bembo

GOGGLES!

EZRA JACK KEATS

VIKING

"Archie, look what I found,"
Peter shouted through the pipe.
"Motorcycle goggles!"
Archie watched Peter through the hole.
He listened and smiled.

Peter ran to the hideout and
put on the goggles.
"Aren't they great?" he asked.
Archie smiled and nodded.

Peter said, "Let's go over
to your house and sit on the steps."
Archie nodded.

They started off.
  Suddenly some big boys appeared.
"Give us those goggles, kid!"
"No, they're mine," Peter said.
  His dog Willie growled.
"Archie, hold Willie," said Peter.

Peter stuffed the goggles into his pocket
and put up his fists.
Archie gasped.
Peter turned to see if something was wrong.

The next thing he knew
he was knocked to the ground.
Everyone stared at the goggles.

Before anyone could move, Willie snatched
the goggles and ran through a hole in the fence.
The big boys chased after him.
"Meet you at the hideout," whispered Peter.
"You go this way, I'll go that way.
   They won't know where we're going.
   Willie will find us!"

Peter raced to the hideout.
He sank down as low as he could.

Footsteps!
"The big boys! They followed me."
Peter held his breath.

ARCHIE!

What was that?

Archie looked through the hole.

There were the big boys—
and there was Willie.
They would see him!

Archie stared at the pipe.
Suddenly he spoke.
"Here, Willie, through the pipe—fast!"

WILLIE!

Peter peeked through the hole.
The big boys were coming—
closer and closer.

Peter took a deep breath.

Then he yelled through the pipe,

"Willie—meet us at the parking lot!"

"Head for the parking lot!" one of the big boys yelled.

"Let's go!"

Peter, Archie and Willie crept out of the hideout.
When they reached the fence they got up and ran.

They got to Archie's house.
  Archie laughed and said,
"We sure fooled 'em, didn't we?"
"We sure did," said Peter,
  handing him the goggles.
"Things look real fine now," Archie said.
"They sure do," said Peter.